A KID'S GUIDE TO FINDING GOOD STUFF

HARBINGER HOUSE
Tucson

WRITTEN AND ILLUSTRATED BY BILL KLEIN

PARENTS AND GROWNUPS,
PLEASE SEE THE NOTE FOR YOU
ON PAGE 64. THANKS!

Published by:
HARBINGER HOUSE
PO Box 42948, Tucson AZ 85733-2948

Edited by Jeffrey Lockridge

Manufactured in the United States of America

2 4 6 8 10 9 7 5 3 1

Library of Congress Cataloging-in-Publication Data
Klein, Bill, 1945-
A kid's guide to finding good stuff / written and illustrated by
Bill Klein
P.   cm.
ISBN 0-943173-96-5 : $11.95
1. Handicraft--Equipment and supplies--Juvenile literature.
2. Salvage (Waste, etc.)--Juvenile literature. 3. Waste products-
-Recycling--Juvenile literature. [1. Recycling (Waste)
2. Handicraft.] I. Title.
TT153.7.K58 1994
745.5--dc20   94-14894

STUFF IN THIS BOOK

TO MY WIFE, GAY
WITH LOVE

IT TAKES A LOT OF UNDERSTANDING
AND PATIENCE TO LIVE WITH A
SCROUNGER !!

WELL, NEVER FEAR!

THE SCROUNGE GANG IS HERE....TO TELL
YOU WHERE TO FIND CLEAN, SAFE, FREE
(OR NEXT-TO-FREE)

GOOD STUFF

FOR MAKING ALMOST ANYTHING
YOU CAN IMAGINE.

LET'S NOT STAND AROUND TALKING.

LET'S GET STARTED!!!

MY TWO BROTHERS AND I WERE LUCKY ENOUGH TO GROW UP IN SMALL TOWNS IN COLORADO. THERE WAS ALWAYS A BACKYARD, AN EMPTY LOT, AND A FRIENDLY NEIGHBOR'S SHED OR GARAGE WITH ALL KINDS OF STUFF LYING AROUND TO GET OUR IMAGINATIONS GOING.

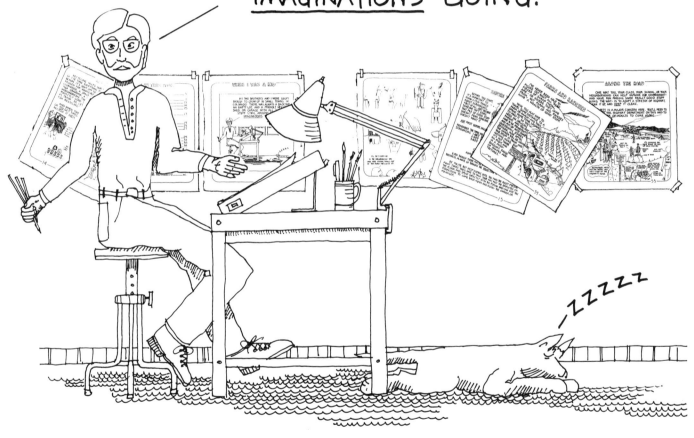

ZZZZZ

JUST BEFORE I STARTED SIXTH GRADE, WE MOVED THE SIX MILES AND SIXTY CURVES FROM CRIPPLE CREEK (WHERE WE'D LIVED THAT SUMMER OVER A BANK AND DOWNHILL FROM A TURQUOISE MINE) TO VICTOR, COLORADO, A MINING TOWN AT THE FOOT OF BATTLE MOUNTAIN.

OUR HOUSE SAT HALFWAY UP THE MOUNTAIN AT 10,000 FEET ABOVE SEA LEVEL, WHERE THE AIR WAS SO THIN IT MADE YOUR LUNGS ACHE.

THERE WE WERE, SURROUNDED BY GOLD MINES THEY'D PULLED MILLIONS OF DOLLARS OF GOLD OUT OF... ONLY ONE DAY EVERYONE – MINERS, MACHINISTS, FOREMEN, ORE CAR PUSHERS, TRUCK DRIVERS, BOOKKEEPERS, BOSSES – HAD JUST STOPPED WORKING, TAKEN OFF, AND NEVER COME BACK!

AND WHAT THEY'D LEFT BEHIND WAS THIS AMAZING COLLECTION OF TOWERS, PLATFORMS, TRACKS WITH SMALL PUSH CARS, HEAVY MACHINERY... MACHINE SHOPS WITH BINS FULL OF PARTS AND ALL SORTS OF METALWORKING MACHINES, OFFICES FULL OF DESKS, CHAIRS, SAFES, AND LEDGER BOOKS, AND STORAGE ROOMS WITH RACKS FULL OF PIECES OF WOOD AND PIPE.

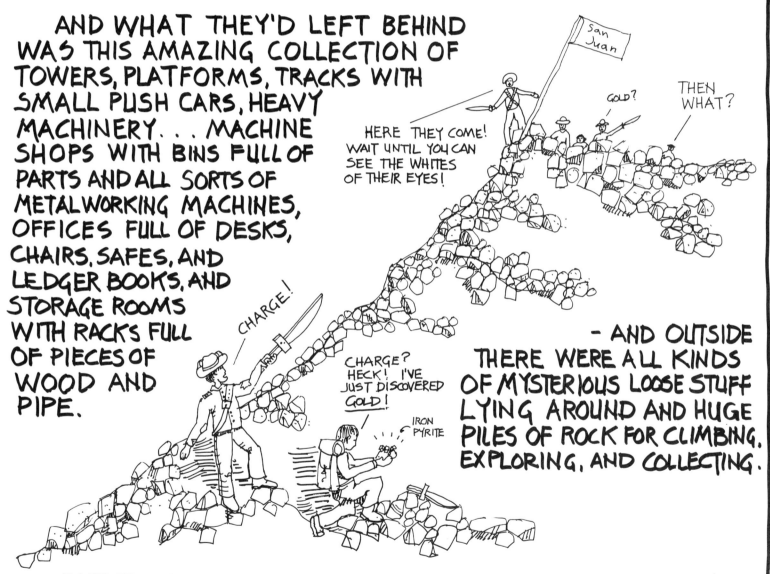

San Juan

HERE THEY COME! WAIT UNTIL YOU CAN SEE THE WHITES OF THEIR EYES!

GOLD?

THEN WHAT?

CHARGE!

CHARGE? HECK! I'VE JUST DISCOVERED GOLD!

IRON PYRITE

– AND OUTSIDE THERE WERE ALL KINDS OF MYSTERIOUS LOOSE STUFF LYING AROUND AND HUGE PILES OF ROCK FOR CLIMBING, EXPLORING, AND COLLECTING.

BUT THE BEST PART WAS, WE LIVED RIGHT NEXT DOOR TO ALL OF IT!

WE PRETENDED TO BE MINERS AS WE PUSHED THE CARS AROUND, WE CLIMBED UNEXPLORED MOUNTAINS, WE ENCOUNTERED ALIENS, WE CHARGED UP AND DOWN!

MY <u>BEST</u> MEMORY IS USING THE LATHES AND MILLING MACHINES AS SUBMARINE CONTROLS AND SAILING THE SEVEN SEAS – AT 10,000 FEET UP!

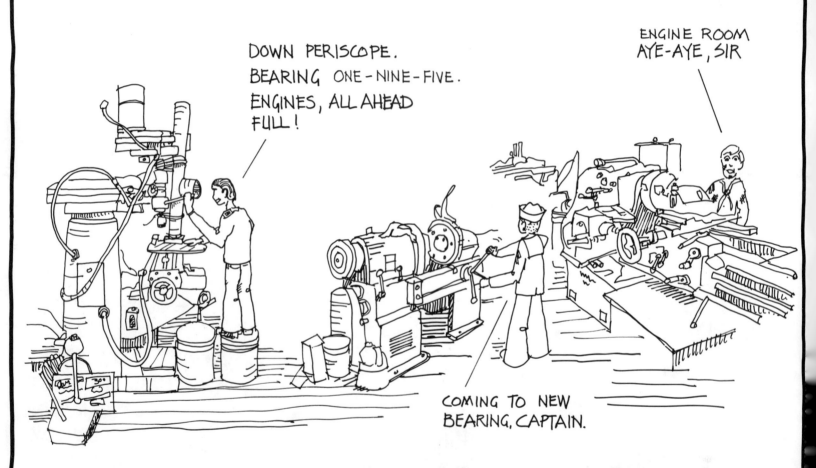

OUR FATHER WORKED WITH MR. CARLTON, THE CARETAKER WHO LOOKED AFTER THE MINING COMPANY'S PROPERTY. WE WERE VERY CAREFUL TO ASK MR. CARLTON'S PERMISSION TO USE SOME OF THE GREAT STUFF THE MINERS LEFT BEHIND. AFTER CHECKING WITH THE OWNERS, HIS ANSWER WAS YES!! AND WE WERE SET FOR YEARS TO COME.

IF WE WERE BUILDING A FORT, OR A RACER, OR A PORTABLE COMBINATION CAMP KITCHEN AND FOOD STORAGE BOX, EVERYTHING WE NEEDED WAS RIGHT THERE FOR THE SCROUNGING. ALL IT COST US WAS OUR TIME AND A LITTLE EFFORT DIGGING AND SORTING THROUGH ALL THE STUFF FOR THE RIGHT PARTS AND PIECES. AND . . . SORTING THROUGH WAS A GREAT WAY TO FIND MORE GOOD STUFF FOR OUR NEXT PROJECT.

YARDS, AT LEAST FOR OUR FAMILY, WERE FOR USING, NOT FOR SHOW. IF WE WANTED TO DIG A HOLE ALL THE WAY TO CHINA, WE DID—ALTHOUGH IN THAT HARD, ROCKY GROUND, WE COULD DIG FOR A WEEK AND BE LUCKY TO GET DOWN A COUPLE OF FEET. (OF COURSE EACH ROCK HAD TO BE EXAMINED FOR GOLD CONTENT AND THAT KIND OF SLOWED US DOWN, TOO)

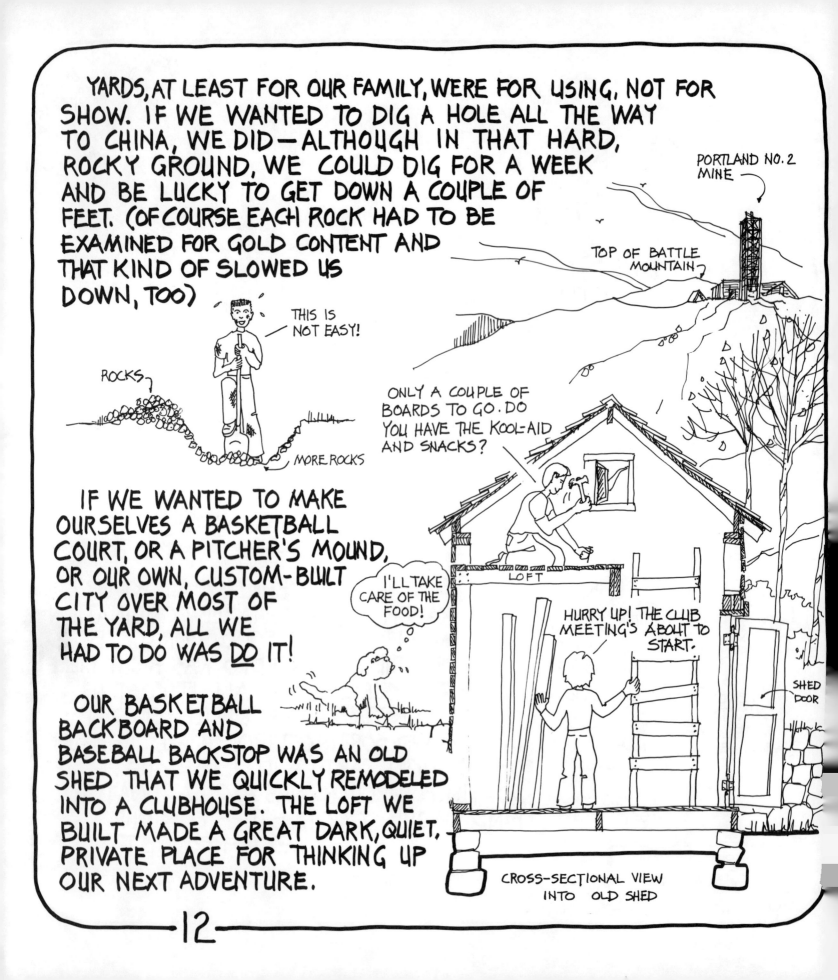

THIS IS NOT EASY!

ROCKS

MORE ROCKS

PORTLAND NO. 2 MINE

TOP OF BATTLE MOUNTAIN

ONLY A COUPLE OF BOARDS TO GO. DO YOU HAVE THE KOOL-AID AND SNACKS?

IF WE WANTED TO MAKE OURSELVES A BASKETBALL COURT, OR A PITCHER'S MOUND, OR OUR OWN, CUSTOM-BUILT CITY OVER MOST OF THE YARD, ALL WE HAD TO DO WAS DO IT!

I'LL TAKE CARE OF THE FOOD!

LOFT

HURRY UP! THE CLUB MEETING'S ABOUT TO START.

OUR BASKETBALL BACKBOARD AND BASEBALL BACKSTOP WAS AN OLD SHED THAT WE QUICKLY REMODELED INTO A CLUBHOUSE. THE LOFT WE BUILT MADE A GREAT DARK, QUIET, PRIVATE PLACE FOR THINKING UP OUR NEXT ADVENTURE.

SHED DOOR

CROSS-SECTIONAL VIEW INTO OLD SHED

12

KIDS TODAY

THERE ARE STILL PLACES IN AMERICA WITH THE KINDS OF GOOD STUFF MY BROTHERS AND I HAD WHEN WE WERE GROWING UP, BUT THEY'RE DISAPPEARING FAST. MOST KIDS DON'T HAVE THE CHANCE TO SCROUNGE AROUND THEIR NEIGHBORHOOD FOR THE PARTS TO MAKE A SIX-WHEELED SUPER-DUPER RACING MACHINE, OR THE BOARDS TO BUILD A TRIPLE-DECKER TREEHOUSE, OR EVEN THE WOOD TO MAKE A MODEL SAIL-BOAT THEY CAN FLOAT ON A STREAM OR A LAKE WHEN THEY GO ON VACATION.

KIDS IN THE SUBURBS, IN BIG CITY HIGH-RISES, OR IN TOWN-HOUSE CONDOS ALL HAVE ONE THING IN COMMON — A SERIOUS LACK OF SAFE, FREE <u>GOOD STUFF</u> FOR BUILDING PROJECTS OR MAKING THINGS.

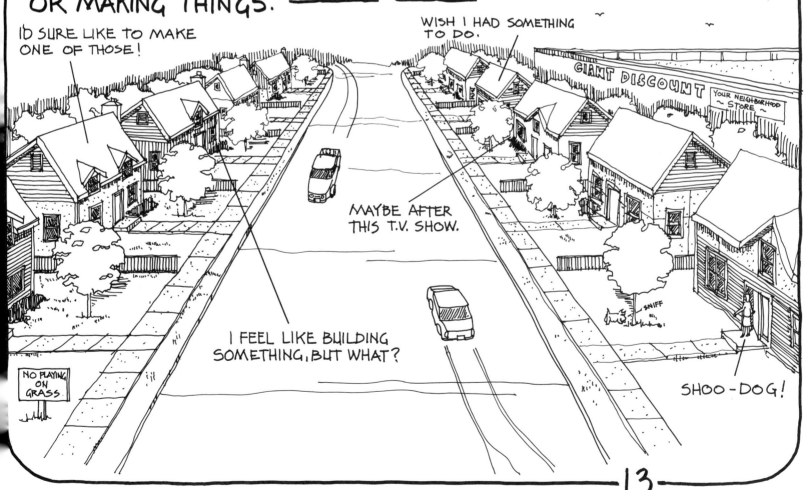

I'D SURE LIKE TO MAKE ONE OF THOSE!

WISH I HAD SOMETHING TO DO.

MAYBE AFTER THIS T.V. SHOW.

I FEEL LIKE BUILDING SOMETHING, BUT WHAT?

NO PLAYING ON GRASS

GIANT DISCOUNT

YOUR NEIGHBORHOOD STORE

SNIFF

SHOO-DOG!

RECYCLING

RECYCLING HELPS OUR ENVIRONMENT—AND IT'S FUN! MOST OF THE TIME EVERYTHING YOU NEED FOR A PROJECT CAN BE RESCUED BEFORE IT'S SENT OFF TO THE LANDFILL OR THE INCINERATOR AND REUSED FOR WHATEVER YOUR IMAGINATION CAN CREATE. A CLUBHOUSE, A SPACE-BOX FORT, A RECIPE BOOK HOLDER FOR YOUR GRANDMA, A METAL SCULPTURE, A TOOLBOX FOR DAD'S WOODWORKING TOOLS—ALL OF THESE CAN BE MADE FROM PERFECTLY GOOD STUFF THAT WOULD HAVE BEEN THROWN AWAY AS TRASH. SO, LET'S GIVE OUR WORLD A BREAK AND HAVE FUN RECYCLING!

AND WHEN YOUR GOOD STUFF GETS TIRED AND WORN OUT —OR YOU GET TIRED OF IT—YOU CAN STILL FIND WAYS TO RECYCLE IT ONE LAST TIME . . .

LET'S TEAR THIS SET DOWN FOR GRANDPA. HE CAN BURN THE WOOD IN HIS STOVE UP AT HIS FISHING CABIN.

I'M TIRED OF THIS MOBILE — I'M GOING TO FEED IT TO THE CAN EATER!

NOW THAT OUR BUG COLLECTION HAS DRIED UP, WHY DON'T WE RECYCLE ALL THESE JARS?

WE REALLY BEAT THESE PLASTIC BOTTLES UP AS FLOATS FOR OUR RAFT. LET'S TAKE 'EM TO THE RECYCLING CENTER.

BEFORE YOU BEGIN

BEFORE YOU START, IT'S IMPORTANT TO KNOW A FEW THINGS ABOUT SCROUNGING. FIRST OF ALL, JUST BECAUSE SOMEONE ISN'T USING THAT PILE OF GOOD STUFF DOESN'T MEAN SOMEONE DOESN'T WANT IT.

<u>ASK</u> FIRST BEFORE DIGGING IN.

REMEMBER THE THREE RULES FOR SCROUNGING 1. GET PERMISSION!
2. GET PERMISSION!
3. GET PERMISSION!

CHAIR FOUND ON THE STREET

LAMP FOUND AT A YARD SALE

ILLUSTRATED DOG USUALLY FOUND UNDERFOOT

DAMAGED DOOR FOUND AT THE BUILDING SUPPLY STORE

SAWHORSE MADE FROM 2x4'S FOUND AT A CONSTRUCTION SITE.

KITCHEN glasses

CABIN BY KLEIN

HOUSE PL

ELEVATIONS

DIVIDED DISH PACKING BOX FOR HOLDING DRAWINGS—FOUND AT NEW NEIGHBOR'S HOUSE

IT'S OFTEN A GOOD IDEA TO HAVE AN ADULT COME ALONG ON YOUR ASKING TRIPS. AND SOMETIMES FINDING OUT WHO TO ASK CAN BE AS MUCH OF AN ADVENTURE AS FINDING WHAT YOU WANT IN THE FIRST PLACE.

EVEN THOUGH THERE MAY BE A WHOLE BUNCH OF GOOD STUFF <u>BEHIND</u> A BUSINESS, ALWAYS GO THROUGH THE <u>FRONT</u> DOOR TO ASK.

BE POLITE BUT KEEP ASKING UNTIL YOU FIND THE RIGHT PERSON. MANY TIMES YOU'LL HAVE TO TALK YOUR WAY PAST THE EMPLOYEE ON THE FLOOR AND SPEAK DIRECTLY WITH THE PERSON WHO CAN GIVE YOU PERMISSION TO COME BACK AGAIN AND AGAIN—THE OWNER OR MANAGER.

AND THERE'LL BE TIMES WHEN YOU <u>WON'T</u> GET PERMISSION TO CART OFF SOME GOOD STUFF. DON'T WORRY, THERE ARE ALWAYS <u>OTHER</u> SOURCES. JUST SMILE, SAY "THANKS ANYWAY," AND HEAD ON OUT TO THE NEXT PLACE.

BEFORE YOU SCROUNGE, MAKE SURE THAT YOUR TETANUS SHOT IS CURRENT AND THAT YOU'RE WEARING GOOD, STURDY WORKMAN'S GLOVES.

LOOK OVER THE STUFF YOU'RE TAKING HOME, AND WATCH FOR SHARP EDGES, NAILS, SPLINTERS, GLOP, AND GOOP.

ALWAYS LOOK FOR GOOD, CLEAN STUFF FIRST. BUT IF THE STUFF YOU WANT NEEDS TO BE CLEANED OFF, TRY TO <u>CLEAN</u> IT UP WHERE YOU FIND IT.

WORK OUT A DEAL WITH MOM AND DAD TO ALWAYS HAVE A STURDY BOX IN BACK OF THE CAR (LARGE PRODUCE BOXES ARE GOOD—THEY'RE MADE OUT OF HEAVY CARDBOARD AND ARE COATED, SO GOOP WON'T SOAK THROUGH).

ALSO, KEEP A SUPPLY OF SELF-SEAL FREEZER STORAGE BAGS OR HEAVY-DUTY PLASTIC GARBAGE BAGS IN THE CAR AND, IF POSSIBLE, SOME OLD NEWSPAPERS OR RAGS FOR WRAPPING YOUR STUFF UP.

ALWAYS KEEP SAFETY IN MIND WHEN LOOKING FOR GOOD STUFF. TAKE AN ADULT ALONG. ASK THE ADULT'S ADVICE. (AND IF IT MAKES SENSE TO YOU, TAKE IT!)

ASK WHOEVER OWNS OR HAS CHARGE OF THE STUFF YOU WANT IF IT'S SURPLUS, AND EXPLAIN TO THAT PERSON WHAT YOU PLAN TO DO WITH IT. MAYBE HE OR SHE WILL SAVE MORE OF IT FOR YOU IN THE FUTURE. BE CAREFUL. HAVE FUN.

SO, AS THE KIDS SAID EARLIER: "LET'S GET STARTED"

THE GRAB-IT-WHEN-YOU-SEE-IT RULE
IS A GOOD ONE TO FOLLOW. IF YOU SEE SOME GOOD
STUFF, DON'T HESITATE! FIND WHOEVER OWNS OR IS
IN CHARGE OF IT AND GET PERMISSION TO TAKE IT.

BOOKSHELVES

DENTED FILE CABINET

BROKEN STOOL

QUICK, LET'S GO HOME AND ASK DAD TO HELP US.

LAWN MOWER

TELEVISION

WOW!

IF YOU SEE SOMETHING YOU WANT, TAKE IT. THE TRASH MAN WILL BE HERE SOON TO HAUL IT AWAY.

CHEST WITH LOTS OF DRAWERS FOR STORING GOOD STUFF

VENETIAN BLINDS

IF IT'S TOO BIG TO CARRY, THEN BEG, BARGAIN, TRADE, OR
COMPROMISE (NO WHINING, PLEASE) WITH YOUR PARENTS (OR WITH
YOUR FRIENDLY NEIGHBORS) TO HAUL YOUR FIND HOME IN THEIR
PICKUP (OR FLATBED TRUCK). BETTER YET, PROMISE YOUR LITTLE
BROTHER A SHARE AND USE HIS WAGON.

IF YOU WAIT, YOU'LL PROBABLY MISS OUT AND FIND SOME-
BODY'S TREATED YOUR GOOD STUFF LIKE TRASH AND TAKEN
IT TO THE DUMP.

ON THE STREET

O.K., THEN YOU'LL HAVE TO LOOK
BEYOND THE HOME FRONT FOR GOOD BUILDING STUFF.

THE STREET'S A GOOD PLACE TO START.

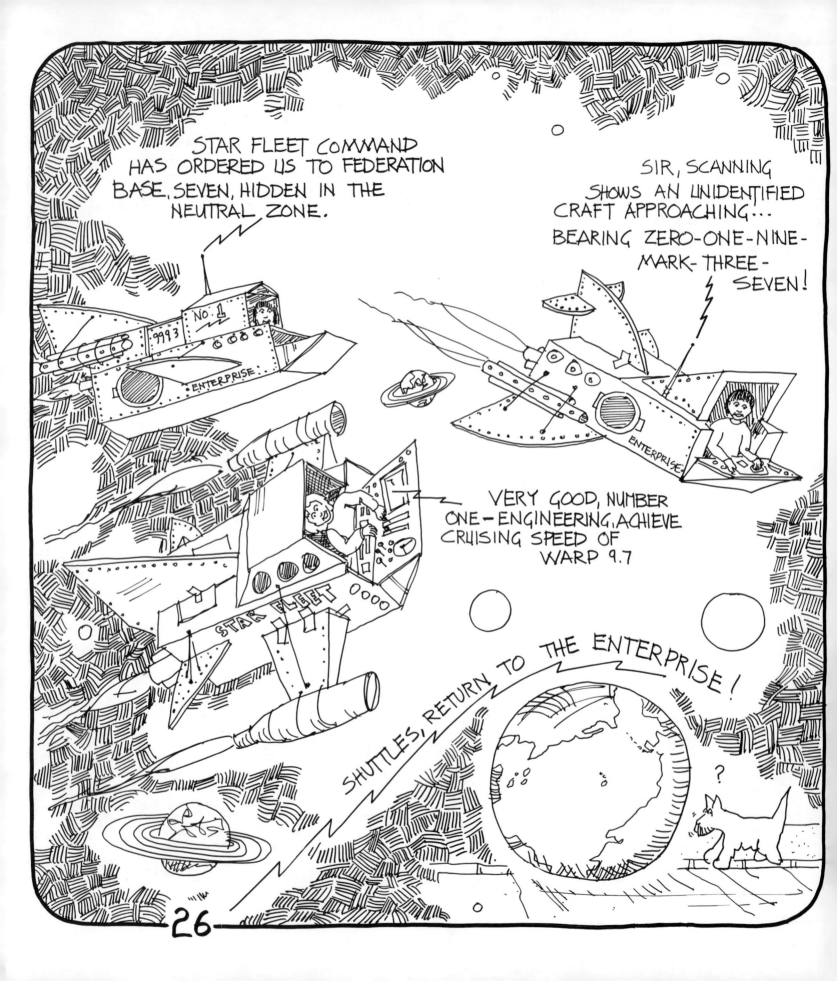

YARD SALE-ING

WHEN YOU'RE LOOKING FOR GOOD, FREE (OR ALMOST FREE) STUFF YOU DON'T USUALLY THINK OF YARD SALES. THE PEOPLE HAVING YARD (OR MOVING OR ESTATE) SALES USUALLY PUT OUT ONLY THE THINGS THEY THINK WILL SELL.

BUT THE STUFF THEY THINK NOBODY WILL BUY— THE GOOD STUFF YOU'RE LOOKING FOR— IS LEANING AGAINST THE SIDE OF THE GARAGE, OR AROUND BACK BEHIND A STORAGE SHED, OR STACKED IN A PILE WAITING TO BE THROWN AWAY.

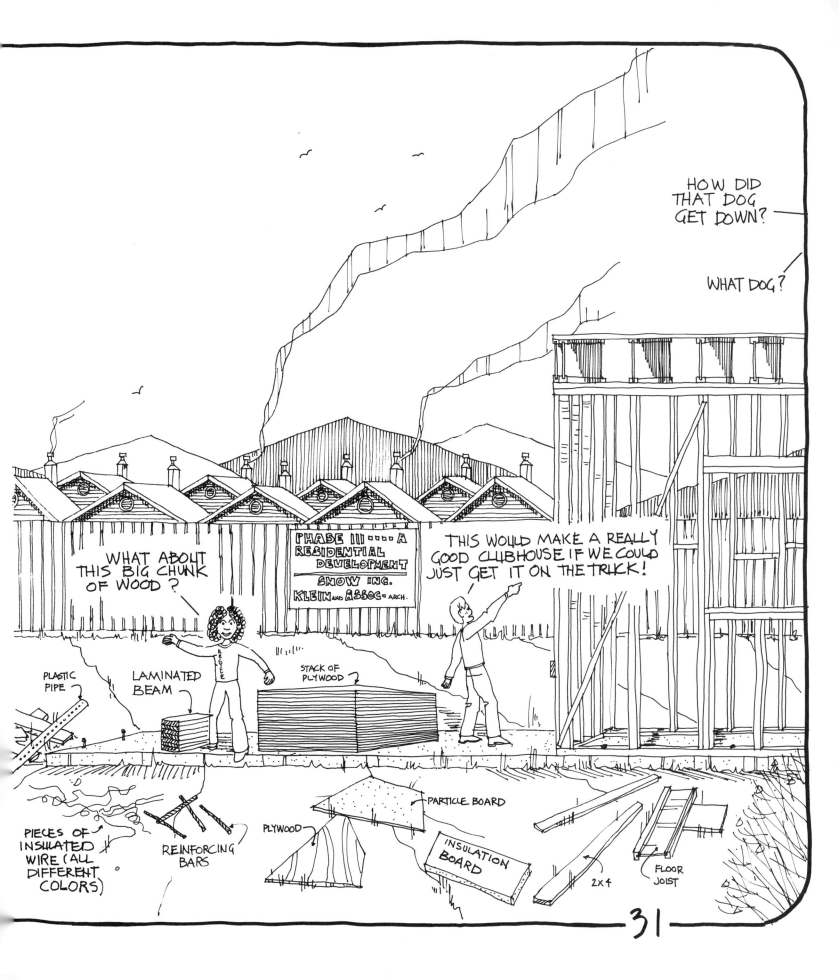

IN THE ALLEY

ALLEYS ARE AMAZING PLACES FOR SCROUNGING. BUT YOU NEED TO USE COMMON SENSE AND A BIG DOSE OF CAUTION WHEN EXPLORING THEM, NO MATTER WHERE YOU LIVE.

ALWAYS TAKE ALONG A PARENT, PICK A SAFE SECTION OF TOWN, AND PLAN TO CHECK THINGS OUT IN BRIGHT DAYLIGHT.

STORES AND MORE STORES

PROBABLY THE BIGGEST AND BEST SOURCE OF GOOD STUFF ARE THE RETAIL STORES THAT ARE AS CLOSE TO YOU AS YOUR NEIGHBORHOOD SHOPPING MALL, OR YOUR DOWNTOWN BUSINESS DISTRICT, OR THE GIANT DISCOUNT SHOPPING CENTER AT THE EDGE OF TOWN. THESE STORES ARE YOUR BEST SOURCE FOR BOXES IN ALL SIZES — AND YOU'D BE AMAZED AT THE GOOD THINGS THEY THROW AWAY!

JUST ASK! THE STORE MANAGER WILL BE GLAD TO HAVE YOU COME AROUND AND LOAD UP.

THE BETTER DISCOUNT FRAME RAY'S COMPUTER GIFT GIANT SALE!

OLD MOVIE POSTERS FROM A VIDEO STORE

BOXES OF SMALL PIECES OF MAT BOARD AND CARPET SAMPLES OR REMNANTS — GOOD, COLORFUL, NEAT, CRISP MATERIALS FOR ART PROJECTS

OLD CASH REGISTERS — GREAT FOR KEEPING TRACK OF YOUR MONOPOLY MONEY

OLD COMPUTER KEYBOARD GREAT FOR YOUR CONTROL BOARD IN YOUR SPACE FORT

VICTOR

REMEMBER, GO THROUGH THE FRONT DOOR, TALK TO THE OWNER OR MANAGER, AND GET YOUR PARENTS TO COME ALONG.

USE COMMON SENSE. YOU'VE GOT A MUCH BETTER CHANCE OF FINDING GOOD STUFF AT FURNITURE STORES, COMPUTER DEALERS, SPORTING GOODS STORES, GIFT SHOPS, PICTURE FRAMERS, AND OFFICE SUPPLY STORES THAN AT SUPERMARKETS, GROCERY STORES, RESTAURANTS, BEAUTY SALONS, AND PET SHOPS — AND WITH A LOT LESS MESS AND HASSLE!

SCROUNGING AROUND THE CITY

AT THE PRINTING COMPANY

WHEN YOU THINK ABOUT IT, A BLANK PIECE OF PAPER HAS MORE PROJECT POTENTIAL THAN ALMOST ANY OTHER MATERIAL YOU MIGHT COME ACROSS IN YOUR SCROUNGING.

THERE IT IS. THE SECRETARY SAID THE MANAGER WAS EXPECTING US.

IT'S GOOD TO KNOW WHERE YOU CAN GET AS MUCH PAPER AS YOU, YOUR FRIENDS, AND YOUR FAMILY CAN HANDLE. PRINTING COMPANIES FILL WASTE CANS WITH CLIPPINGS, CUTTINGS, AND TRIM PIECES OF ALL KINDS OF SHAPES, COLORS, TEXTURES, AND WEIGHTS. SOMETIMES, IF YOU'RE REALLY LUCKY, THE PRINTERS WILL BE DISCONTINUING A CERTAIN TYPE OF PAPER AND YOU COULD GO HOME WITH A STACK OR TWO OF BRAND-NEW PAPER. THE POSSIBILITIES ARE ENDLESS.

AGAIN IT'S IMPORTANT TO GO IN THE FRONT WAY—ESPECIALLY HERE! SOMETIMES WHAT GOES OUT THE BACK DOOR WILL BE COVERED WITH WET INK THAT COULD REALLY MESS UP YOUR AFTERNOON.

HERE YOU GO, KIDS.

WOW! WE STRUCK IT RICH.

THIS IS JUST LIKE BRAND NEW. THANKS!

SAVE FOR SCROUNGE GANG

TAKE A PARENT, A FRIEND WITH A STRONG BACK, OR A REALLY GOOD WAGON BECAUSE THIS STUFF CAN BE HEAVY. AND IF YOU DROP BACK BY ON A REGULAR BASIS, YOU MAY GET THE MANAGER TO SET ASIDE THEIR SCRAPS JUST FOR YOU!

-39-

I'LL BET EVERY KID IN THE NEIGHBORHOOD WAS OVER HERE MAKING THINGS OUT OF THAT PAPER THEY GAVE US.

PRETTY COOL!

AT THE ARCHITECT'S OFFICE

CHIRP

HI, KIDS! COME ON IN!

THANKS

HI, COOL OFFICE

THEY SAID THEY HAD A BUNCH OF TILE AND CARPET SAMPLES FOR US.

LET'S GO GET THEM!

G.S.

RECYCLE

ARCHITECTS' OFFICES ARE USUALLY GOLD MINES OF GREAT STUFF. SALES REPRESENTATIVES ARE CONSTANTLY BRINGING THEM NEW SAMPLES OF WALL PAPER, TILE, WOOD, CARPET, AS WELL AS PAINT CHIPS, PLASTIC LAMINATE, AND RUBBER BASE. THE OUTDATED SAMPLES ARE SENT BACK TO THE DISTRIBUTOR, WHO THROWS THEM AWAY— OR THEY'RE TOSSED INTO THE ARCHITECT'S WASTE-PAPER BASKET. ALL YOU HAVE TO DO IS ARRANGE FOR THE ARCHITECT TO SET THEM ASIDE FOR YOU AND THEN PICK THEM UP ON A REGULAR BASIS.

BACKSTAGE AT THE THEATER

A FUNNY THING HAPPENED ON THE.....

PART OF THAT SET WOULD WORK GREAT AS A FORT IN OUR BACKYARD. LET'S ASK MOM AND DAD, AND THEN FIND OUT HOW TO GET IT!

COOL!

HAVE YOU EVER WONDERED WHAT HAPPENS TO THAT NEAT SET IN THE PLAY YOU SAW LAST WEEK AT THE LOCAL THEATER, ONCE THE SHOW IS OVER, THE LIGHTS ARE OFF, AND THE ACTORS HAVE MOVED ON? SOME ITEMS ARE SAVED AND STORED — LAMPS, CHAIRS, TABLES, BOOKSHELVES, STAGE TREES — TO BE RECYCLED FOR SEASONS TO COME.

BUT THAT ROMAN STREET SET, OR THAT ENGLISH DRAWING ROOM SET, OR THAT LOG CABIN SET — WHAT ABOUT IT? IT TOOK THE STAGE CREW A LONG TIME TO MAKE, OUT OF GOOD, EXPENSIVE MATERIALS, BUT ALL TOO OFTEN IT WINDS UP IN THE LOCAL LANDFILL — UNLESS YOU RESCUE IT! A THEATER SET IS SOMETHING KIDS, PARENTS, TEACHERS ALL COULD PUT TO GOOD USE IN THE BACKYARD, REC. ROOM, OR CLASSROOM.

MOST SETS ARE BUILT ONLY TO LAST THROUGH THE PLAY. EVEN THOUGH THEY APPEAR SOLID AND THREE-DIMENSIONAL, THEY'RE REALLY FLAT—AND THEREFORE EASY TO TAKE APART AND MOVE.

AN ADULT WITH A BIG TRUCK WOULD COME IN REAL HANDY FOR THIS PROJECT.

IF YOU'RE MOVING THE SET TO YOUR GARAGE CLUBHOUSE OR EVEN THE BACKYARD, MAKE A DEAL WITH YOUR PARENTS — YOU'LL ONLY USE THE SET FOR A CERTAIN TIME, THEN YOU'LL TEAR IT DOWN AND REUSE THE MATERIALS FOR BUILDING OTHER THINGS.

47

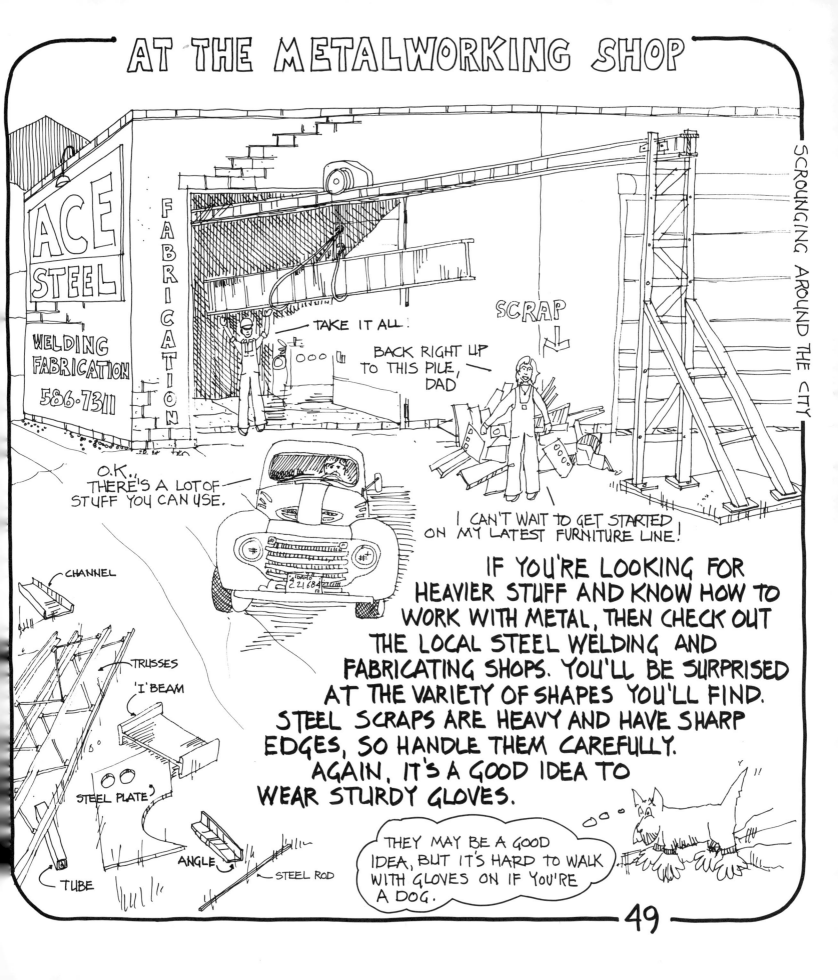

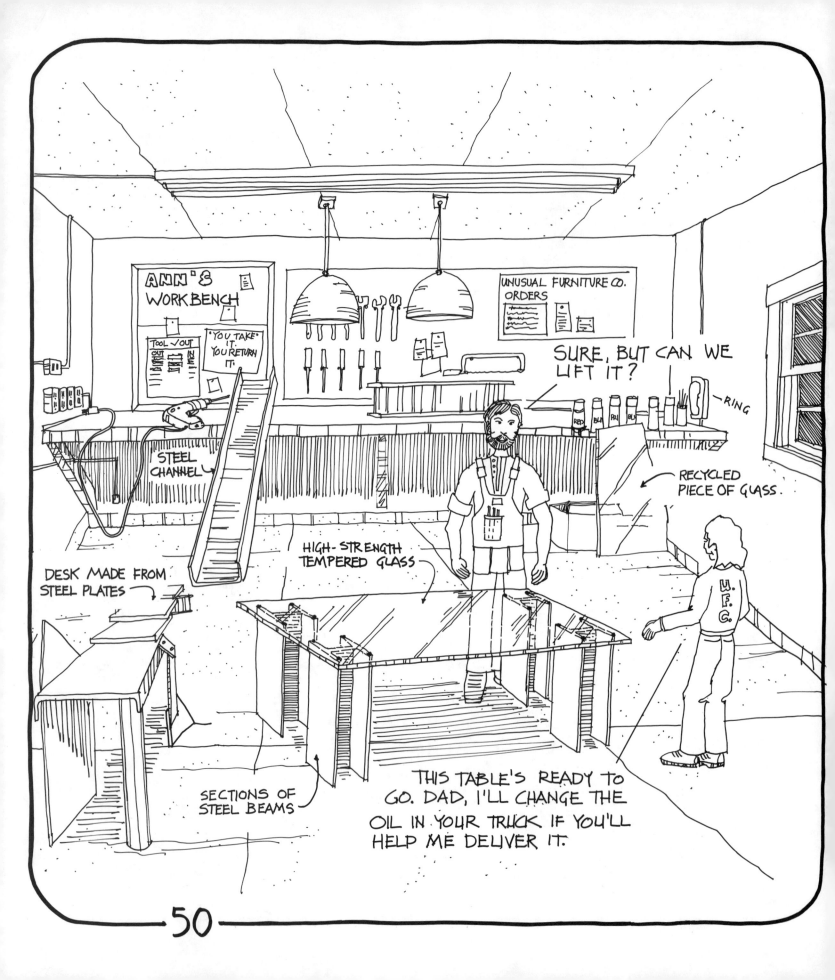

THE WOODWORKER'S WORLD

WOOD IS ALWAYS GOOD TO LOOK FOR. IT'S USUALLY FOUND IN SMALL PIECES, IT'S CLEAN, AND IT'S RELATIVELY EASY TO WORK WITH. JUST ABOUT EVERYONE HAS WOODWORKING TOOLS, SO THEY'RE EASY TO BORROW. REMEMBER, ASK PERMISSION FIRST, AND CLEAN AND RETURN TOOLS AS SOON AS YOU CAN TO THE SAME PLACE WHERE YOU FOUND THEM.

PROFESSIONAL CABINET MAKERS DON'T END UP WITH MUCH SURPLUS, BUT THEY WILL HAVE SMALLER PIECES OF OAK, CHERRY, BIRCH, AND OTHER MORE EXOTIC WOODS.

THEIR SHOPS ARE OFTEN LOCATED IN THE INDUSTRIAL AREA OF TOWN, SO IT'S A GOOD IDEA TO TAKE AN ADULT ALONG. LOOK IN THE YELLOW PAGES FOR ADDRESSES AND PHONE NUMBERS, AND BE SURE TO CALL AHEAD.

SCROUNGING AROUND THE CITY

FINE ERIC' CA

LET ME GET THIS LOADED, AND WE'LL TAKE A LOOK.

O.K., UP IT GOES

NICE-LOOKING CABINETS!

HEY, ERIC, DO YOU HAVE ANY WOOD SCRAPS WE COULD HAVE?

THERE ARE MANY OTHER SOURCES OF WOOD YOU MIGHT INVESTIGATE. IF YOU LIVE NEAR A SAWMILL, THEY USUALLY HAVE A PILE OF SCRAP WOOD, CALLED "MILL ENDS," THAT THEY'LL LET YOU HAVE BY THE PICKUP FULL FOR A SMALL FEE.

THE PIECES ARE SHORT AND ROUGH, BUT THEY WORK FINE FOR MANY THINGS.

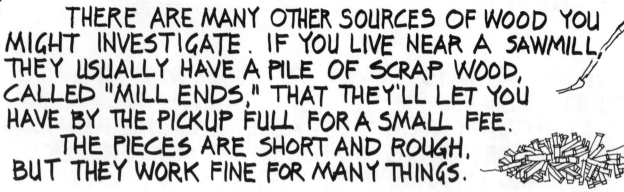

TRUCK TAKING WOOD CHIPS TO BE RECYCLED

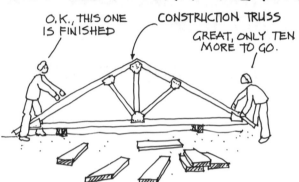

O.K., THIS ONE IS FINISHED

CONSTRUCTION TRUSS

GREAT, ONLY TEN MORE TO GO.

ALSO, CHECK THE YELLOW PAGES FOR A LOCAL CONSTRUCTION TRUSS MANUFACTURER.

THEY DON'T HAVE A LOT OF WASTE, BUT WHAT THEY DO HAVE IS STRAIGHT AND CLEAN.

HIGH SCHOOLS, VOCATIONAL SCHOOLS, COLLEGES, AND UNIVERSITIES — IF THEY OFFER SHOP OR BUILDING CLASSES — ARE ALSO GREAT SOURCES OF GOOD STUFF. CALL AND FIND OUT.

GREAT! ARE THERE MORE PIECES OF WOOD? I'D LIKE YOU TO SHOW ME HOW YOU DID THAT.

NOW THAT I'VE LEARNED HOW TO DO OIL PAINTINGS, I'M GOING TO MAKE AN OAK FRAME FOR MY FIRST MASTERPIECE.

MORE WOOD COMING UP

THIS HOT GLUE GUN IS GREAT FOR STICKING ALL THESE SCRAPS TOGETHER. LIKE MY DESIGN?

CAREFUL! THAT GLUE IS HOT AND STICKY.

I HOPE MY LITTLE BROTHER LIKES THE CAR I'M MAKING HIM.

ALONG THE ROAD

ONE WAY YOU, YOUR CLASS, YOUR SCHOOL, OR YOUR NEIGHBORHOOD CAN HELP IMPROVE OUR ENVIRONMENT— AND HAVE FUN FINDING SOME REALLY GOOD STUFF ALONG THE WAY—IS TO ADOPT A STRETCH OF HIGHWAY, CLEAN IT UP, AND <u>KEEP</u> IT CLEAN.

<u>SAFETY</u> IS A MAJOR CONCERN HERE. YOU'LL NEED TO WORK WITH THE HIGHWAY DEPARTMENT ON THIS AND TO GET A NUMBER OF ADULTS TO COME ALONG.

NOW, YOU MAY HAVE TO CONVINCE THE ADULTS THAT WHAT YOU'VE FOUND IS VALUABLE FOR A FUTURE ART PROJECT, RATHER THAN JUST TRASH TO BE THROWN AWAY.

SO, AS YOU PICK UP CANS, PAPER SLIPS, BOTTLES, AND OTHER LITTER, KEEP YOUR EYES OPEN FOR SOME GOOD STUFF.

EVEN IF YOU DON'T SEE AN IMMEDIATE USE FOR IT, SQUIRREL IT AWAY, THINK ABOUT IT, AND SOMEDAY INSPIRATION WILL HIT!

WOW! YOU MADE THIS SCULPTURE OUT OF THAT OLD PIECE OF METAL?

REALLY COOL. HOW'D YOU DO IT?

WELL, I DIDN'T HAVE TO DO MUCH TO THE SHAPE OF THE BODY AND WINGS.
I CLEANED IT UP, SCREWED ON THE HEAD, AND PAINTED IT FLAT BLACK.
I CALL IT THE BLACK SWAN!

I'VE NEVER BEEN ABLE TO FIGURE OUT WHAT ALL THOSE PIECES OF SCRAP METAL ARE — OR WHERE THEY CAME FROM, BUT FARMS AND RANCHES HAVE A WEALTH OF GOOD STUFF.

NOW, YOU MAY HAVE TO TRAVEL SOME DISTANCE TO A FARM OR RANCH — AND THEN SPEND SOME TIME LOOKING — TO FIND IT. SO YOU'LL NEED AN OBLIGING PARENT. AND YOU MAY HAVE TO BE PERSISTENT AND PUT UP WITH SOME QUESTIONING STARES BECAUSE, MOST OFTEN, THE OWNER WILL BE CONVINCED YOUR STUFF IS TRASH AND NOTHING MORE. BUT IT'S OUT THERE ALL RIGHT, AND IN A MIND-BOGGLING RANGE OF SHAPES AND TEXTURES.

WAY OUT AND ABOUT

THERE'S THE HOUSE!

PUFFERIDGE TREE FARMS
BALDY MT. ROAD

FORD

THERE'S ONE MORE PILE OF GOOD STUFF OVER HERE

THE PTA IS LOOKING FOR TIRES FOR THEIR NEW PLAYGROUND PROJECT.

THIS SHOULD DO IT.

I'D LIKE TO TAKE ONE OF THESE HOME AND HANG IT OVER MY BEDROOM DOORWAY.

GOOD IDEA! HANG IT ENDS UP, AND LUCK STAYS IN.

HANG IT ENDS DOWN... AND LUCK FALLS OUT.

HORSESHOE

YOKE

FEEDING GEAR FROM A CORN PLANTER

CONNECTOR BETWEEN THE HANDLE AND THE BLADE ON A SCYTHE

SCROUNGERS...

LOOK, SOMEONE IS THROWING AWAY THAT PATIO CHAIR.

OUR WORLD IS FULL OF GOOD STUFF (SOMETIMES CALLED TRASH BY OTHERS) JUST WAITING TO BE RE-CYCLED INTO WHATEVER OUR IMAGINATIONS CAN MAKE OF IT.

QUICK, LET'S GRAB IT!

NOW YOU KNOW A BUNCH OF PLACES TO GET GOOD STUFF AND YOU'VE GOT SOME IDEAS OF WHAT TO DO WITH IT ONCE YOU RESCUE IT FROM GOING TO THE LANDFILL OR DUMP, OR FROM THE BACK OF GRANDPA'S SHED.

I WANT TO MAKE SOMETHING REALLY DIFFERENT WITH THIS... BUT WHAT?

BUT WHAT IF YOU'RE SEARCHING FOR SOMETHING DIFFERENT, SOMETHING UNIQUELY YOURS TO MAKE OR BUILD? HOW DO YOU _FIND_ THAT SOMETHING?

START YOUR ENGINES!

WELL, FIRST OF ALL, RELAX AND LET YOUR MIND ROAM. IF YOU NEED TO, STASH YOUR GOOD STUFF IN A SAFE PLACE— OUT OF EVERYONE'S WAY. TAKE A WALK, READ A BOOK. DON'T WORRY, YOUR IMAGINATION IS CRANKING AWAY. ALL YOU HAVE TO DO IS TO GIVE IT TIME.

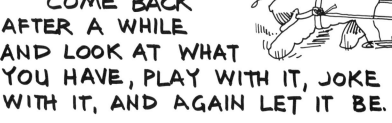

COME BACK AFTER A WHILE AND LOOK AT WHAT YOU HAVE, PLAY WITH IT, JOKE WITH IT, AND AGAIN LET IT BE.

SUDDENLY, WHEN YOU <u>LEAST</u> EXPECT IT, IT'LL COME TO YOU! SOMETHING ONLY YOU AND YOUR NEAT STUFF COULD MAKE! IT'S A GREAT FEELING!

HAPPY SCROUNGING !!!

NOTE TO PARENTS AND GROWNUPS

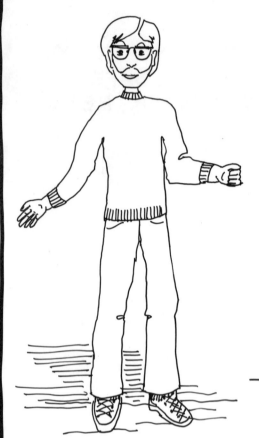

FINDING GOOD STUFF—SCROUNGING—WORKS BEST AS A <u>JOINT</u> VENTURE BETWEEN ADULTS AND CHILDREN. WITH A LITTLE PLANNING <u>BEFOREHAND</u> —AND A HEALTHY DOSE OF COMMON SENSE— SCROUNGING CAN BE SAFE, REWARDING, AND FUN FOR EVERYONE INVOLVED.

TAKE TIME TO LEAF THROUGH THE BOOK. SOME OF THE SUGGESTIONS AND SOURCES WILL BE MORE APPROPRIATE FOR YOUR FAMILY (OR COMMUNITY), SOME LESS. YOU'LL KNOW (ESPECIALLY AFTER CHECKING THINGS OUT) WHICH PLACES AND SOURCES IN YOUR COMMUNITY ARE SAFE AND FUN BESIDES, AND WHEN YOUR KIDS WILL NEED YOUR HELP —AND YOUR CAR OR TRUCK—TO HAUL THEIR <u>GOOD</u> <u>STUFF</u> HOME.

WORK OUT CLEAR, SENSIBLE GROUND RULES WITH YOUR KIDS AS TO WHAT THEY CAN AND CANNOT BRING HOME— ALSO HOW AND WHEN. ENCOURAGE THEM TO TALK THINGS OVER WITH YOU <u>BEFORE</u> THEY GO OUT SCROUNGING. HELP THEM PUT TOGETHER AN OFFICIAL SCROUNGERS' KIT (SEE PAGE 16) THAT WILL NOT ONLY PROTECT THEM AND THEIR GOOD STUFF BUT ALSO THE INSIDE OF YOUR CAR OR TRUCK.

SCROUNGING LETS YOU AND YOUR KIDS EXPLORE NEW PLACES (OR NEW PARTS OF OLD ONES), ENGAGE IN HANDS-ON RECYCLING, STRETCH YOUR IMAGINATIONS — AND HAVE A LOT OF FUN!

HAPPY SCROUNGING! Bill Klein